Dear Parent:

Congratulations! Your child is taking the first steps on an exciting journey. The destination? Independent reading!

STEP INTO READING® will help your child get there. The program offers five steps to reading success. Each step includes fun stories and colorful art. There are also Step into Reading Sticker Books, Step into Reading Math Readers, Step into Reading Write-In Readers, Step into Reading Phonics Readers, and Step into Reading Phonics First Steps! Boxed Sets—a complete literacy program with something for every child.

Learning to Read, Step by Step!

Ready to Read *Preschool–Kindergarten*
• big type and easy words • rhyme and rhythm • picture clues
For children who know the alphabet and are eager to begin reading.

Reading with Help *Preschool–Grade 1*
• basic vocabulary • short sentences • simple stories
For children who recognize familiar words and sound out new words with help.

Reading on Your Own *Grades 1–3*
• engaging characters • easy-to-follow plots • popular topics
For children who are ready to read on their own.

Reading Paragraphs *Grades 2–3*
• challenging vocabulary • short paragraphs • exciting stories
For newly independent readers who read simple sentences with confidence.

Ready for Chapters *Grades 2–4*
• chapters • longer paragraphs • full-color art
For children who want to take the plunge into chapter books but still like colorful pictures.

STEP INTO READING® is designed to give every child a successful reading experience. The grade levels are only guides. Children can progress through the steps at their own speed, developing confidence in their reading, no matter what their grade.

Remember, a lifetime love of reading starts with a single step!

Copyright © 1999 by Raymond Briggs. Illustrations by Maggie Downer, based on the book
THE SNOWMAN by Raymond Briggs. All rights reserved under International and
Pan-American Copyright Conventions. Published in the United States by Random House
Children's Books, a division of Random House, Inc., New York, and simultaneously in Canada
by Random House of Canada Limited, Toronto.

www.stepintoreading.com

Educators and librarians, for a variety of teaching tools, visit us at
www.randomhouse.com/teachers

Library of Congress Cataloging-in-Publication Data
Knudsen, Michelle.
Raymond Briggs' The snowman / adapted by Michelle Knudsen ; [illustrated by Maggie
Downer]. p. cm. — (Step into reading. A step 1 book)
SUMMARY: When his snowman comes to life, a little boy invites him home and in return is
taken on a flight high above the countryside.
ISBN 0-679-89443-8 (trade) — ISBN 0-679-99443-2 (lib. bdg.)
[1. Snowmen—Fiction.] I. Briggs, Raymond. Snowman. II. Downer, Maggie, ill. III. Title.
IV. Series: Step into reading. Step 1 book. PZ7.K7835 Rau 2003 [E]—dc21 2002013783

Printed in the United States of America 20

STEP INTO READING, RANDOM HOUSE, and the Random House colophon are registered trademarks
of Random House, Inc.

STEP INTO READING®

STEP 1

RAYMOND BRIGGS'
The Snowman

adapted by Michelle Knudsen

Random House 🏠 New York

Hooray!
It is
snowing!

James gets dressed.

He runs outside.

He makes a pile of snow.

He makes it
bigger

and

bigger.

He puts a big snowball
on top.

He adds a scarf
and a hat.

He adds an orange
for a nose.

He adds coal
for eyes and buttons.

There!

What a fine snowman!

It is nighttime.
James sneaks downstairs.

He looks out the door.

What does he see?

The snowman is moving!

James invites him in.

The snowman has never
been inside a house.

Hello, cat!

Hello, lamp!

Hello, paper towels!

The snowman

takes James's hand.

They go up, up,
up into the air!

They are flying!

What a wonderful night!

It is morning.

James jumps out of bed.

He runs downstairs.

He runs into the kitchen.

He runs outside.

But the snowman
has gone.